My dear mouse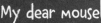

Have I ever told you how much I love science fiction? I've always wanted to write incredible adventures set in another dimension, but I've never believed that parallel universes exist . . . until now!

That's because my good friend Professor Paws von Volt, the brilliant, secretive scientist, has just made an incredible discovery. Thanks to some mousetropic calculations, he determined that there are many different dimensions in time and space, where anything could be possible.

The professor's work inspired me to write this science fiction adventure in which my family and I travel through space in search of new worlds. We're a fabumouse crew: the spacemice!

I hope you enjoy this intergalactic adventure!

Geronimo Stilton

PROFESSOR PAWS VON VOLT

THE SPACEMICE

GERONIMO STILTONIX

TRAP STILTONIX

THEA STILTONIX

GRANDFATHER WILLIAM STILTONIX

ROBOTIX

BENJAMIN STILTONIX AND BUGSY WUGSY

...tilton

SPACEMICE

AWAY IN A
STAR SLED

Scholastic Inc.

Copyright © 2014 by Edizioni Piemme S.p.A., Palazzo Mondadori, Via Mondadori 1, 20090 Segrate, Italy. International Rights © Atlantyca S.p.A. English translation © 2016 by Atlantyca S.p.A.

The publisher does not have any control over and does not assume any responsibility for author or third-party websites or their content.

GERONIMO STILTON names, characters, and related indicia are copyright, trademark, and exclusive license of Atlantyca S.p.A. All rights reserved. The moral right of the author has been asserted. Based on an original idea by Elisabetta Dami. www.geronimostilton.com

Published by Scholastic Inc., *Publishers since 1920*, 557 Broadway, New York, NY 10012. SCHOLASTIC and associated logos are trademarks and/or registered trademarks of Scholastic Inc.

Stilton is the name of a famous English cheese. It is a registered trademark of the Stilton Cheese Makers' Association. For more information, go to www.stiltoncheese.com.

No part of this publication may be reproduced, stored in a retrieval system, or transmitted in any form or by any means, electronic, mechanical, photocopying, recording, or otherwise, without written permission of the copyright holder. For information regarding permission, please contact: Atlantyca S.p.A., Via Leopardi 8, 20123 Milan, Italy; e-mail foreignrights@atlantyca.it, www.atlantyca.com.

This book is a work of fiction. Names, characters, places, and incidents are either the product of the author's imagination or are used fictitiously, and any resemblance to actual persons, living or dead, business establishments, events, or locales is entirely coincidental.

ISBN 978-1-338-03286-4

Text by Geronimo Stilton
Original title *La magica notte delle stelle danzanti*
Cover by Flavio Ferron
Illustrations by Giuseppe Facciotto (design) and Daniele Verzini (color)
Graphics by Francesca Sirianni

Special thanks to AnnMarie Anderson
Translated by Anna Pizzelli
Interior design by Kevin Callahan / BNGO Books

10 9 8 7 6 5 4 3 2 1   16 17 18 19 20

Printed in the U.S.A.   40

First printing 2016

In the darkness of the farthest galaxy in time and space is a spaceship inhabited exclusively by mice.

This fabumouse vessel is called the **MouseStar 1**, and I am its captain!

I am Geronimo Stiltonix, a somewhat accident-prone mouse who (to tell you the truth) would rather be writing novels than steering a spaceship.

But for now, my adventurous family and I are busy traveling around the universe on exciting intergalactic missions.

THIS IS THE LATEST ADVENTURE OF THE SPACEMICE!

A Very Special Speech

It all began one day before **dawn**. Yes, you read that correctly: before dawn! Even though I'm usually the kind of mouse who can sleep until **noon**, that morning I woke up very, very early. I headed right to my desk without even changing out of my pajamas. I **ABSOLUTELY** had to finish working on something very **IMPORTANT**! It was no **easy** task, though. In fact, for forty-five stellar minutes, I **GNAWED** on my laser pen as I tried to think of something to write!

Oh, I'm so sorry! I haven't introduced myself. My name is Stiltonix, **Geronimo Stiltonix**, and I am the captain of the *MouseStar 1*, the most mouserific spaceship in the whole universe. Honestly, though, my real dream is to become a writer!

As I was saying, I was working on a very important assignment when my personal robot assistant, **ASSISTATRIX**, burst into my cabin as he does every morning.

"**Wake up, wake up, wake** — what?" he said in surprise. "But you're already awake, Captain!"

"Uh, that's right," I replied. "I'm working on my speech for the ***NIGHT OF THE DANCING STARS*** party!"

You might be wondering what that is. **Well,**

I'll tell you! It's the event everyone has been looking forward to for **months**!

Every year, there is a wonderful night when the stars **DANCE** around the **universe**, painting colorful trails behind them in the sky. On this magical night, the jolly **elfix** — citizens of the planet **TWINKLIX** — fly their star sled across the universe, bringing beautiful presents to everyone. It's a night full of *joy*, friendship, and happiness, and we **spacemice** celebrate by exchanging small gifts and throwing an enormouse party!

In other words, the Night of the Dancing Stars is the most beloved holiday in the **Cheddar Galaxy** . . . actually, in the entire **universe**!

As captain of the *MouseStar 1*, I had to prepare a very **special** speech for that

From the Encyclopedia Galactica
THE NIGHT OF THE DANCING STARS

The elfix work all year to make gifts for every creature in the universe. On the Night of the Dancing Stars, they fly all over the galaxies in a giant star sled adorned with tiny silver bells, delivering presents to the four corners of the universe.

From the Encyclopedia Galactica
THE ELFIX

Home Planet: Twinklix, a planet shaped like a wrapped package

Specialty: Making beautiful gifts

Motto: **"Away in a star sled we go, bringing gifts to all we know!"**

very special night. But Assistatrix wasn't listening. My personal assistant robot just carried on with his usual morning routine.

"Captain Stiltonix, it's time to wash up!" Assistatrix ordered. **"Wash up! Wash up! Wash up!"**

I sighed. It was no use fighting that **STUBBORN** little robot. So I stepped into the **Wash-O-Mouse** for my morning shower.

"You know what, Assistatrix?" I said as I stepped out of the Wash-O-Mouse after it was finished. "A nice warm shower with a **lunar cheese**-scented bath gel was just what I needed! Now I'm ready to focus on my spee — **AAAAAHHHHHH!**"

I had stepped right on a **SLIPPERY** bar of solar soap. I slipped all over my cabin like a spaceship trying to avoid an incoming asteroid.

Galactic Gorgonzola! What bad luck!

I was just about to slam my snout into the cabin door when Assistatrix grabbed me by my bath towel and lifted me into the air.

"This is not the time to go skating, Captain," he ordered. "*Get dressed! Get dressed! Get dressed!*"

He pushed me toward my closet, and I quickly got dressed.

Heeeeeelp!

Swish

"Captain, you're late for the party rehearsal!" Assistatrix THUNDERED. "Run, run, run! Everyone is waiting for you at the Space Yum Cafe!"

I raced out of my cabin in a DAZE and hailed an astrotaxi. An astrosecond later, I was ZOOMING toward the spaceship's restaurant.

THERE'S SO MUCH TO DO!

I walked into the Space Yum Café and found it *BUZZING* with energy and excitement. A few spacemice were decorating the room with *lights* and *ribbons* while others were busy wrapping gifts. And another group of spacemice was busy in the kitchen, baking delicious **cheesy** desserts for their friends and families to enjoy.

My sister, Thea, spotted me and ran over.

"Geronimo!" she exclaimed. "Are you ready? You have a lot of work to do! You have to take a look at all the DECORATIONS, listen to the intergalactic chorus rehearse, and choose the **color** scheme for the party!

Do you prefer **galactic green** or **moldy Gorgonzola green**?"

I hesitated. "Er, what's the difference?"

Thea ignored me and **chattered** on.

"And that's just the beginning — there's so much to do!" she squeaked as she unrolled a really **LOOOOOOONG** list!

I groaned. **Why**, **why**, **why** was it always up to me to decide everything? Maybe it was because I am the captain of the ship. **Sigh!**

"Hey, Cuz," my cousin Trap greeted me. He was holding a box of yummy-looking sweets. "These three-cheese chocolates are really **DELICIOUS**!"

I reached out to try one, but he moved the box away **faster** than a cat chasing a mouse.

"**PaWS OFF!**" he scolded. "You have so much to do already . . . **I'LL** take care of

Paws off!

sampling the desserts for the banquet buffet!"

He CHUCKLED as he walked away.

"Geronimo, did you prepare the elfix welcome speech?" Thea asked.

Stellar Swiss! I still had to finish my speech!

I was about to reply when another voice squeaked up.

"*Grandson, look sharp!*" my grandfather, Admiral William Stiltonix, thundered. "Don't slouch! Try to welcome our friends the elfix with some dignity. *Don't make me look bad!*"

"G-g-good morning, Grandfather," I replied. "**Of course** I will treat our guests well! After all, I am the ship's captain!"

"Well, I should hope so!" Grandfather barked. Then he started shouting orders at me.

Luckily, at that moment, *Sally de Wrench* arrived. She is the *MouseStar 1*'s official mechanic and technician, and she is the loveliest and smartest rodent on the ship. Every time I see her, my brain turns to BRIE! Ah, what a fascinating mouse! I wanted to get her a thoughtful gift for the Night of the Dancing Stars, but I was completely STUMPED on an idea.

"Earth to Geronimo!" Grandfather scolded me. "Are you listening to me? It's like you're not even *PAYING ATTENTION*!"

"S-sure I am, Grandfather," I squeaked.

"Now, I'm afraid you'll have to **excuse me** . . ."

I quickly hurried away. I just had to find my friend **Professor Greenfur**, the ship's resident scientist. He would know the **P E R F E C T** gift for Sally!

It has to be the perfect gift!

THE TAIL TWISTER
2000

Professor Greenfur was probably in his laboratory, working on some new EXPERiMENT. When I walked in, I found him and my nephew Benjamin studying a really STRANGE contraption: It looked like something halfway between a **lawn mower** and a fur-curling iron.

"Hi, Uncle G!" Benjamin greeted me. "Did you come to admire Professor Greenfur's latest invention?"

"Hi, Benjamin," I replied as I gave my adorable

nephew an enormouse hug. "Uh, yes . . . Nice invention, Professor. It's truly incredible! But, er . . . **What is it?**"

"Good morning, Captain!" Professor Greenfur exclaimed as he tightened a few screws. "May I present my most recent invention: the **Tail Twister 2000**!"

I still had no idea what the thing was!

"Wow!" I exclaimed. "It's fabumouse. But . . . uh, what do you *do* with it?"

"That's easy," he replied. "This invention will **REVOLUTIONIZE** life on board the *MouseStar 1*! It can cut, curl, shave, twist, or braid any tail, anytime! We still have to test it out, but —"

"Let's remedy that **right away**!" Trap exclaimed as he sauntered into the lab holding a Pluto cheese sandwich.

STINKY SPACE CHEESE! Whenever Trap

gets involved, I'm the one who gets into *trouble*!

Before I could stop him, my cousin **grabbed** the Tail Twister 2000.

"Let's try this thing, Ger!" Trap said enthusiastically. "In just a few seconds, I'll give you a really modern **SPACE TAILSTYLE**!" He pressed the button, and the Tail Twister 2000 began to *buzz* loudly.

BLACK HOLEY GALAXIES! That contraption

pinched my entire tail! A second later, Trap stepped back and smiled, looking very Pleased with himself.

"Ta-da! What a **mousterpiece**!" he said.

I turned to take a look.

Solar-smoked Gouda! My tail was completely *curled*! I looked ridiculous. That tail certainly was not fit for the **CAPTAIN** of a spaceship! I wanted to C R Y.

What?!

Ta-da!

3. . . . and twisted it into an enormouse curl!

"Isn't it great?" Trap said with a chuckle. "Don't you know that curls are the **LATEST FASHION** in the whole galaxy?"

"There's nothing to **laugh** about, Trap!" I replied.

Out of the corner of my eye, I could see that Professor Greenfur and Benjamin were **LAUGHING**, too.

I was about to return to my cabin with my **curly** tail between my legs when Hologramix, the *MouseStar 1*'s computer, appeared in front of me, yelling:

"Yellow alert!
Yellow alert!
Yellow alert!"

Mousey meteorites! What could have happened?

I MIGHT TOSS
MY CHEESE . . .

We all raced out of the lab and headed toward the **control room**.

"Hurry, Uncle G!" Benjamin squeaked. "Something serious must have happened."

He was right: The yellow alert kept getting **LOUDER** and **LOUDER**!

"Let's take the *liftrix*!" Professor Greenfur suggested.

Oh no! Not the liftrix! Do you know what the liftrix is?

It's a big GLASS TUBE that transports passengers on the *MouseStar 1* from one floor to another. It uses a very strong

Heeeeeeeeelp!

jet of air to lift mice up or lower them down to the desired floor.

Every time I use it, I get off with my whiskers **TREMBLING** and my stomach in my throat. I was about to suggest taking an **astrotaxi** instead when Trap grabbed me and pushed me into the liftrix.

"Let's goooo!" he shouted.

A stream of air

LIFTED us and pushed us up as if we were missiles headed toward a faraway planet. When I got off, I felt like I was about to **toss my cheese**! I will never, ever, ever get used to the liftrix!

Ugh! I feel so sick!

INTERSTELLAR
INTERFERENCE

As soon as we arrived in the **control room**, Grandfather William began scolding me.

"Geronimo!" he exclaimed. "Where have you been? Didn't you hear the YELLOW ALERT? A yellow alert means you have to get to the control room **RiGHT awaY**. I mean **iM—ME—Di—ate—LY**! In fact, you should have been here before you even HEARD the alert!"

Huh? How was that even possible?

I was about to reply when Grandfather continued.

"And **what in the name of cheddar**

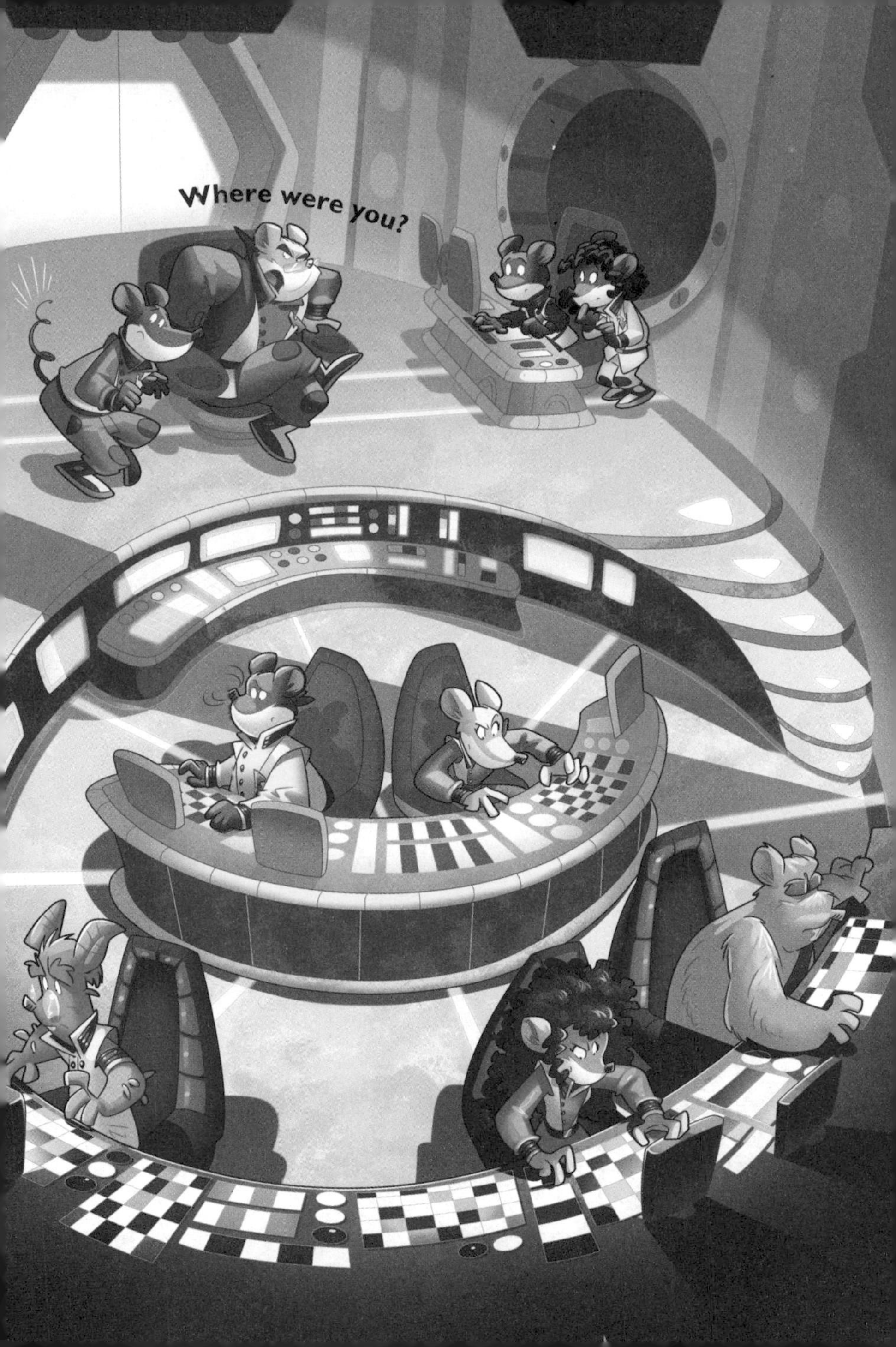
Where were you?

happened to your **tail**?" he squeaked.

"Uh, well, you see —" I began, but he cut me off.

"Not now, Geronimo!" Grandfather bellowed at me. "We don't have time for chitchat. There's a very **serious** problem!"

Great galaxies! My whiskers **trembled** with worry, and it wasn't just because of the serious problem. I had just noticed Sally de Wrench **STARING** at my curled tail!

HOW EMBARRASSING!

Luckily, my sister, Thea, brought me back to the present.

Uh . . .

"Geronimo, the situation is really serious," she said gravely. "We have received a **MYSTERIOUS** message from Twinklix."

"**TWINKLIX?**" I gasped. "Are the elfix in trouble? Let's listen to the message **right away**!"

"Of course, Captain," Sally replied. "But the message isn't very **clear**. We seem to be experiencing some **interstellar interference**."

"Huh?" I asked.

"Our sound system's **functionality** is not ideal," Sally explained.

I still didn't have a **CLUE** what she was talking about. Thea must have seen it on my snout.

"Basically, there's a lot of **STATIC**, Geronimo," my sister explained.

Sally pressed the button to play the

message, but all we heard was:

BZZZZZZZZZZZZZ...

"Ugh!" Trap groaned, putting his paws over his ears. "What an AWFUL sound! I couldn't understand a thing!"

"Clearly we need to stabilize the sound input and adjust the MAGNETIC WAVES," Hologramix chimed in.

I looked at the computer blankly. But I didn't want Sally to know I was clueless again!

"Well, why didn't you say so?" I said instead. "Sally, please stabilize the sound input and **adjust** the magnetic waves!"

Sally nodded and immediately started **pushing** buttons and **FLIPPING** switches.

"There!" she exclaimed. "Now the sound system should work!"

The reception was still fuzzy, but we were finally able to make out some of the message:

"H-h-help! Bzzzz...bzz...W-w-we are...bzz...bzz...prison...bzz!"

The message stopped abruptly.

"*We are prison?*" Trap asked. "What does that mean?"

"I think it means 'we are **prisoners**'!" Benjamin squeaked.

The room became **SILENT**. You could have heard a slice of cheese drop. It sounded like the elfix had been elf-napped!

A Mission for the Spacemice!

We were all stunned. Our friends the elfix were in TROUBLE — it sounded like they were being held against their will! But who had taken them? And why? And, most importantly, what were we going to do about it?

"We have to head to Twinklix right away!" Thea exclaimed. "That way we can figure out what happened and what we need to do next. This is a mission for the spacemice!"

"Thea is right," Professor Greenfur agreed. "We can't waste any time. The elfix may be in danger!"

"We're coming, too!" **BENJAMIN** and Bugsy Wugsy shouted together. "We want to help you save the elfix."

We're coming, too!

I hated to disappoint them, but I shook my head.

"I'm sorry, but you two can't come along," I explained gently. "It might be DANGEROUS!"

Benjamin and Bugsy Wugsy looked crestfallen.

"Well, I could stay on the spaceship with them . . ." Trap offered slyly.

Martian mozzarella!

My cousin was trying to get out of going on

31

the mission with us! That sneaky rat.

Thankfully, Grandfather William set Trap straight.

"I don't think so, Trap!" Grandfather bellowed. "We'll need EVERYONE on board to help save the elfix — including you. And of course Geronimo will be the commander of the expedition. After all, he is the captain of the *MouseStar 1*!"

GULP!

Grandfather was right, but I was still as scared as a mouse being chased by a cat!

"Of course I'll lead the expedition," I squeaked, trying to sound more confident than I felt. "But who — or what — are we looking for?"

"Captain Stiltonix is right!" Professor Greenfur exclaimed. "We don't know who took the elfix, or why! The elfix are such sweet and **gentle** creatures. Everyone in the cosmos LOVES them. What in space could have happened?"

"There's only one way to find out," Thea replied **firmly**. "We must leave for Twinklix right away!"

GULP!

If only I was as **BRAVE** and **courageous** as my sister, Thea!

A Real Captain Does the Right Thing

We started planning the mission to Twinklix **immediately**. I had no idea what to expect when we arrived. Would we come **snout-to-snout** with giant blue aliens with purple tentacles when we landed our spaceship? Or would spotted green aliens with enormouse teeth **attack** us? *Who knew?*

Help!

My whiskers **shook** with fear. I really don't like going on dangerous missions —

I just want to be a writer!

"Geronimo," Grandfather William said seriously. "There is a time to **SIT BACK** and watch, and there is a time to **take action**. A real captain does the right thing."

Solar Swiss! Grandfather was right. I knew what I had to do: save the elfix!

Just then Sally asked, "Captain, are you ready to be **teletransported**?"

"Absolutely," I replied as confidently as I could. Then I bravely stepped onto the Teletransportix platform along with Thea, Trap, and Professor Greenfur. I closed my eyes and took a *deep breath* . . .

I really **don't like** being teletransported

Huh?

around the galaxy. I'm afraid I'll lose some *whiskers* or the TIP OF MY NOSE or an entire ear during the molecular transfer. Yikes! I opened my eyes again, relieved that the transfer was over. But I was shocked: We hadn't moved an inch!

Yikes!

Ahhhh!

"What's going on?" Trap snapped grumpily.

"I don't know," Sally replied. "It's very WEIRD."

Then she pressed the Teletransportix switch for the second time.

"STILL NOTHING!" Thea said.

36

Sally tried one more time . . .
Still no luck!

"It looks like the Teletransportix is broken," Sally said.

Professor Greenfur examined the machine carefully.

"It's not the Teletransportix!" he announced. "It looks like something is **blocking** the atmosphere and Twinklix. That's why we can't teleport ourselves. We have to find a **different** way to get there!"

PHEW! I was relieved. Now I wouldn't have to worry about my whiskers! But I had another problem: How would we get to Twinklix?

"I know!" Thea chimed in. "We can take my **space pod**!"

"Great plan," Sally said. Then she smiled

right at me. "**Good luck with the mission, Captain!**"

My fur turned as red as a cheese rind. **Did this mean she liked me?**

I said good-bye to Benjamin and Bugsy Wugsy and climbed into the space pod with Thea, Professor Greenfur, and Trap. Moments later, we were on our way to **TWINKLIX**.

Good luck!

See you soon!

LET THE MISSION BEGIN!

During the *flight*, Professor Greenfur organized his scientific equipment. He had brought **a lot** of it with him!

"Do you really think we'll need all that stuff, Professor?" I asked.

"Well, you never know," he replied. "I'd rather be prepared for anything. After all, we might encounter fur-eating *microorganisms*, intergalactic INSECTS, or **pirate spacecats**! There are so many dangerous things in the Cheddar Galaxy."

How scary!

Galactic Gorgonzola! D-d-dangerous?
I began to *shake* and turned as **pale** as
lunar mozzarella.

"Hey, Cuz, stop **shaking**
so much!" Trap scolded
me. "The space pod is
lurching back and forth.
I can't get any sleep!"

He yawned loudly and
leaned back in his seat,
closing his eyes.

"How can you **sleep**
right now?!" I asked,
exasperated.

But then Thea got on my
case, too.

"Trap's right, Ger!" she squeaked. "This
shaking is **distracting** me from
driving!"

So I tried to sit **CALMLY** in my seat. One positive thing was that the *curling* effect of the Tail Twister 2000 had worn off — my tail was back to normal!

We continued to cruise through space until we heard a **strange** buzzing sound.

"What's that sound?" Thea asked.

ZZZZZZZ . . .

"It's just Trap," I replied. "He's snoring!"

Bzz . . . bzz . . . bzz . . . Zzzzzzzz . . .

"No, Trap's snoring is getting mixed in with another sound in the background," Professor Greenfur explained. "Can't you **hear** it?"

Bzz . . . bzz . . . bzz . . . Zzzzzzzz . . .

The professor was right: What could it be?

"Trap, wake up!" Thea shouted.

Only then did I realize where the

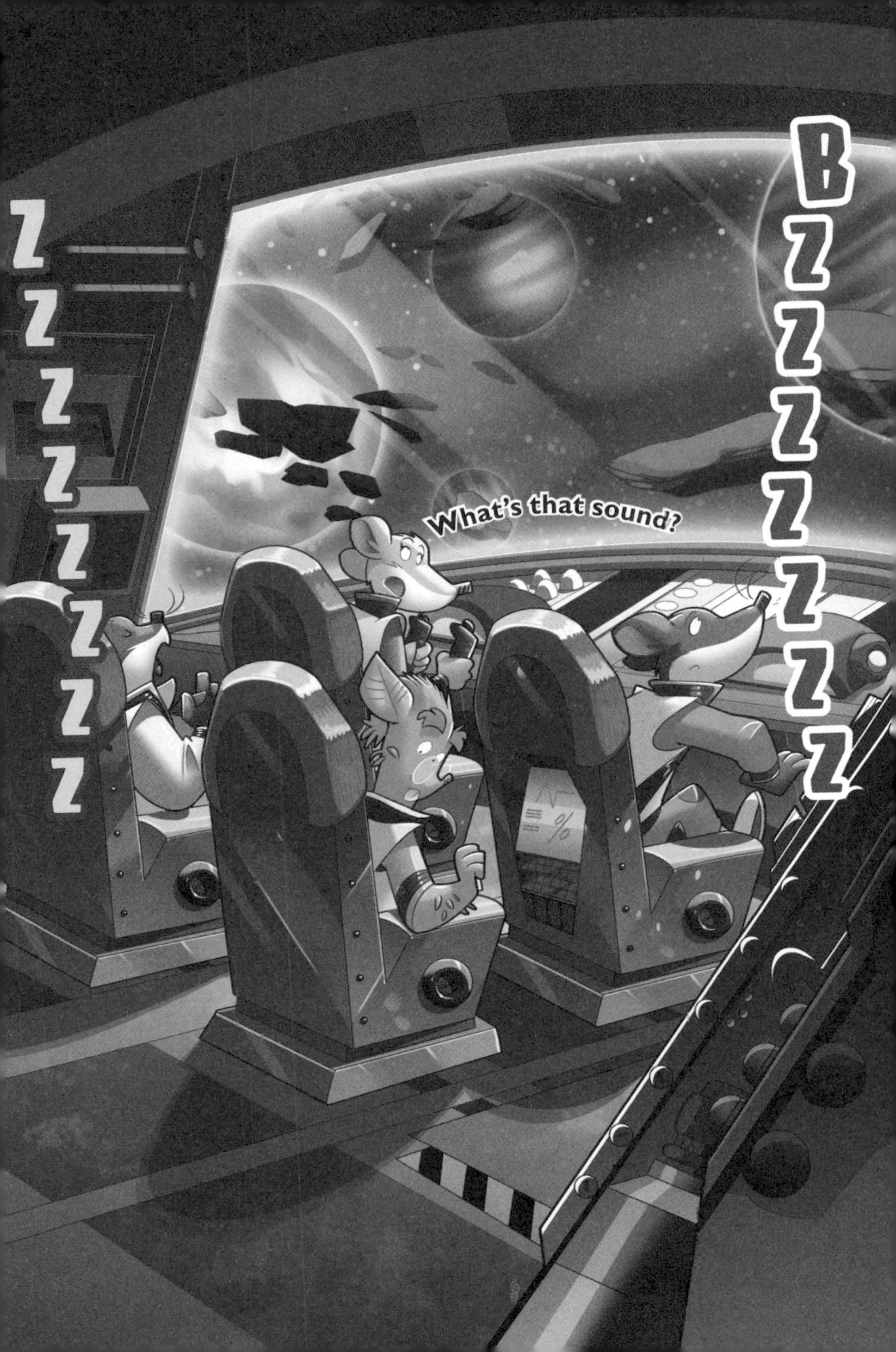
ZZZZZZZZ
What's that sound?
BZZZZZZZZ

SOUND was coming from: my wrist phone! It was **vibrating** loudly.

"It's me!" I exclaimed. "There's a call coming through!"

I answered the call with a push of a *button*.

"Hello?" I squeaked.

Even though the connection was **terrible**, I could hear Sally's voice faintly: "Captain Stiltonix, Captain Stiltonix . . . **BZZ BZZ** . . . I have finally managed to **BZZ BZZ** . . . get in touch with —"

"What was that?" I asked. "There's a lot of **static**!"

"Captain, can you hear me?" Sally continued. "The connection isn't working properly. It's as if there is an **energy field** blocking the **BZZ . . . BZZ . . .**"

The buzzing sound cut her off again. It was the same type of interstellar interference we had heard in the *control room* when we were trying to listen to the elfix's message.

"Captain, Captain!" Sally said loudly. "It will be hard to get another connection, so please listen CAREFULLY. There's someone else on Twinklix in addition to our elfix friends."

"Someone else?!" I shouted. "But who?"

There was **no reply**: My wrist phone had suddenly turned off. But thanks to my shouting, Trap was finally awake.

"What's going on?" he yelped. "Who woke me up? Did I miss anything?"

"Yes, you missed the entire flight!" Thea said with a sigh. "Now we're getting very close to TWINKLIX. Prepare for arrival!"

THE PLANET TWINKLIX

I had never **SEEN** Twinklix, but I had read in the *Encyclopedia Galactica* that it was a beautiful planet covered in brightly COLORED plants.

But when we landed, I was shocked. Everything was dark and gray. There was no color anywhere!

"How strange!"

Professor Greenfur exclaimed.

TWINKLIX

The space pod had landed near a village made up of **small** houses with **pointy** roofs. The houses were decorated with **round** wreaths.

But instead of the **bright colors** that we had seen in the *Encyclopedia Galactica*, everything here was **DULL**. Plus, the village was shrouded in a damp, **foggy** mist.

What was going on?

How strange!

We took a few steps forward, but we couldn't **see** a thing.

Suddenly, we heard a loud sound from near our space pod.

Crash!

"W-what was that?" I stuttered.

Was it a scary alien from Venus?
A horrible, fur-eating monster?

A dangerous mutant space vegetable?

The space pod door creaked open slowly.

"Uncle G!" squeaked a tiny voice.

I breathed a sigh of relief: It was Benjamin and Bugsy Wugsy!

"What are you two doing here?" I asked. "I told you this mission was too dangerous!"

Uncle G!

It's you!

"We want to help the **elfix**, too," Bugsy Wugsy explained.

"Plus, we want to be with you, Uncle!" Benjamin added.

I was touched. The mouselings' BRAVERY reminded me that I needed to be brave, too.

"Okay, you can come," Thea said. "But no more stowing away! You have to stay with us all the time. Trap, grab the flashlights!"

"Uh, how many are there supposed to be?" Trap asked. "I only see TWo."

"There should be FOUR," I reminded him. "Didn't you pack them?"

"I thought you were doing it!" he replied. "After all, you are the captain!"

I was about to reply when my sister cut us off.

"We don't have time to **argue**!" Thea

said in exasperation. "We have to find the **elfix**!"

You were supposed to do it!

No, it was your job!

So we began to walk through the **deserted** village. Trap and I held the flashlights, but they didn't **illuminate** much. We could barely see two pawsteps in front of our snouts!

Suddenly, Professor Greenfur STOPPED walking. I was right on his tail, and I crashed into him.

"**OUCH!**" I squeaked. "What is it? What's happening? Why did you stop?"

"Captain, I see **pawprints**!" he replied.

PAWPRINTS IN THE DARK!

Pawprints?! Trap pointed his FLASHLIGHT at the ground, where we could clearly see an enormouse **pawprint** on the planet's sandy surface.

Holey craters! My tail curled up in fear. Those pawprints were much too BIG to belong to the elfix.

"LOOK!" Thea exclaimed, pointing ahead. "There are more. Let's follow them and see where they lead."

"**F-F-FOLLOW THEM?**" I stuttered, my whiskers **trembling**. "A-are you s-s-sure that's a g-good idea?"

Before we could make up our minds, the flashlights suddenly **went off**.

I almost **JUMPED** out of my fur.

"What's going on?" I asked, worried. I **checked** one of the flashlights, and it suddenly *turned back on*, shining right in my snout!

Then, two astroseconds later, the **light** went out again.

"There must be some sort of

What's going on?!

interstellar interference in this area," Thea pointed out. "That's probably why our **equipment** isn't working very well."

Suddenly, I was very aware that we were on an unusual planet at the edge of the cosmos in the complete **dark**. Squeak! I was so scared, my **fur** was standing on end!

Then I realized I hadn't heard Benjamin or Bugsy Wugsy **SQUEAK** in a while.

"Benjamin?" I called out. "Bugsy Wugsy?"

"We're right **here**, Uncle," Benjamin replied.

"Great!" I said, trying to sound more confident than I felt. "Stay close."

A light ahead of us caught my attention — it looked like a **flashlight**!

"Nice work, Trap!" Thea exclaimed. "How

did you fix the flashlights?"

"Uh . . . well, to be honest, I didn't do *anything*!"

The next thing I knew, I saw **two**, **four**, **Six**, **eight** more lights go on!

Galactic Gorgonzola! Those lights couldn't have been our flashlights, because we only had **two** of them!

I soon realized what they were. The bright lights that had looked like flashlights were really the **EYES** of some mysterious aliens!

Caught!

I gulped. The aliens were looking at us **threateningly**.

"Back to the spaceship, quick!" Thea yelled. "Come on! Run!"

But the aliens didn't intend to let us get away. They SET OFF after us faster than a falling meteor, caught us, and **tied** us up tightly like we were *NIGHT OF THE DANCING STARS* gift packages!

We weren't able to MOVE a whisker. Then the aLiENS picked us up and

Run!

carried us each away. It was **pitch-black**.

Stinky space cheese! A thousand questions crowded my mind:

1. Who were these mysterious aliens?

2. Where were they taking me?

And most importantly . . .

3. Where were my friends?

Then I heard the sound of a door opening, and a dim light flooded the space. From the corner of my EYE I could see Thea, Trap, and Professor Greenfur. We were in a large room with a haRDWooD floor. But there was no sign of Benjamin and Bugsy Wugsy!

At least we could get a clear look at the aliens who had **MOUSENAPPED** us.

They were enormouse! Their gray fur was matted and tangled, and they had gigantic fangs hanging from their mouths.

I glanced at Professor Greenfur to see if he seemed familiar with the species. But he looked as shocked as I was! I noticed that each alien had a **dark little ball** at the tip of its tail.

How strange!

Then a large, husky alien came toward me. He seemed like the **BOSS**. He looked me up and down carefully.

"What mouseoid species are you?" he asked menacingly. "We want to know **WHY** you came here and **WHAT** you want!"

"We are spacemice," I replied, trying my best to sound **firm** and **BRAVE**. "My name is Geronimo Stiltonix, and I am the captain of the **MouseStar 1**! These are my shipmates. We are here because we received a message from our friends the elfix asking

for our help! Now, **WHO** are you? And what are you doing on Twinklix?"

"We are the **nebulos**, and we come from the planet **Nebula**," he growled in reply. "My name is **NEGATIVIX**, king of the nebulos. We have invaded Twinklix and captured all the elfix. Hee, hee, hee!"

"But **WHY**?" Thea asked. "And where are our friends now?"

Negativix burst out laughing.

"Oh, they're safe!" he replied. "But we had to imprison them! You see, the **elfix** never bring us any gifts! Year after year passes, and they've never come to Nebula. Not even once! So we decided to come get the gifts ourselves. And to make up for lost years, we're forcing the elfix to make presents for **US** and only **US**!"

"But surely there's been a mistake,"

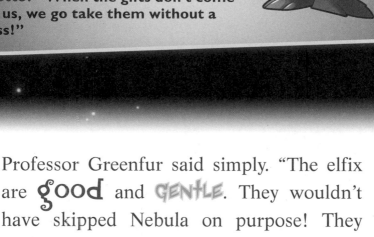

From the Encyclopedia Galactica

THe NeBULOS

Home Planet: Nebula

Personality: Bad-tempered and obnoxious

Distinguishing Mark: Each alien has a mysterious dark ball at the tip of its tail.

Motto: "When the gifts don't come to us, we go take them without a fuss!"

Professor Greenfur said simply. "The elfix are good and GENTLE. They wouldn't have skipped Nebula on purpose! They drive their star sled all over the universe, delivering gifts to everyone."

But Negativix just shook his head.

"What I say is true," he replied. "We poor nebulos have never received anything from the elfix."

"But couldn't you have talked to them first?" Thea suggested. "You didn't have to **imprison** them!"

"Enough!" Negativix growled. "It's too late now. And we can't let you get in the way of our plan. Guards, take these spacemice to **prison** immediately!"

He signaled to two aliens behind him. We tried to fight back, but the nebulos were much **bigger** and **STRONGER** than we were. They lifted us and carried us **down** a steep staircase. Then one guard opened the door to a room with many cells. The other alien tossed us into a cell and **locked** it behind us.

We were in big trouble!

A BRAVE
LITTLE ELFIX

The situation was as prickly as a Plutonian thorn bush: We were in a **DARK** cell with **iron** bars all around us and no way out!

"Now what do we do?" Trap asked, sounding discouraged.

Thea sat next to him on the floor, looking worried.

"We're in big **TROUBLE**," she said with a sigh.

"And where are Benjamin and Bugsy Wugsy?"

Holey space cheese! What were we going to do?

"I'm sure Benjamin and Bugsy Wugsy are okay," Professor Greenfur said reassuringly. "We just need to come up with an escape plan!"

The cell was silent as we all tried to think.

"It won't be easy," said a soft, gentle voice, breaking the silence.

"Who's that?" I replied. "Is someone there?"

"Who, me?" came the reply.

We all looked around the cell carefully. There in the corner was a *tiny* creature with light green skin and a nose shaped like a small trumpet. He was wearing a cap, a long jacket, and a pair of light green pants.

"Martian mozzarella!" Professor

Greenfur exclaimed. "It's an elfix!"

The creature smiled.

"That's right," it said in a **SWEET** and musical voice. "I'm Rubix, and I'm a toymaker."

"My name is Thea Stiltonix," my sister said, holding out a **paw**. "It's very nice to meet you!"

"We are *spacemice*," I explained further. "We are good friends of the elfix. Every year, we appreciate your **generous** gifts. We received a message that you were in trouble, and we came as quickly as we could. Where are the other **elfix**?"

My name is Rubix!

Rubix sighed sadly. Then he told us the whole story.

"The nebulos aliens invaded our planet and forced us to make gifts just for them," he explained. "They haven't received gifts for years, and now they don't want to share with anyone! My friends are WORKING hard at the toy lab."

"But why didn't you bring the nebulos any gifts?" Thea asked, a puzzled look on her snout. "That seems very unlike the kind elfix."

"We didn't do it on purpose!" Rubix explained. "The planet Nebula is always enveloped by thick, DARK fog. So we didn't even know it existed! I tried to explain that to Negativix, but he didn't believe me."

NEBULA

"What a SAD tale!" I replied as Rubix wiped away a tear.

"Now my friends and family are being forced to work for the nebulos aliens," he continued with a sigh. "And Twinklix is **GRAY** and **dull** because the nebulos have so many negative feelings."

"Don't worry!" Thea said encouragingly. "WE'LL hELP YOU SOMEhOW!"

Trap still looked confused.

"But why are you locked up in this cell with us instead of making toys with your friends?" my cousin asked.

"It's because I rebelled," Rubix replied **proudly**. "I didn't want to make gifts just for the nebulos. Every inhabitant of the galaxy deserves something **SPECIAL**!"

Solar-smoked Gouda! What a brave little elfix!

My friends and I **looked** at one another.

I'm a rebel!

"It's time to take action!" I ordered my crew.

Thea smiled and nodded.

"SPACEMICE FOR ONE, SPACEMICE FOR ALL!" we cheered loudly.

RESCUED!

Rubix looked at us gratefully.

"Thank you, friends!" he said warmly. "But I have one *very small* question . . ."

"Yes?" Trap replied.

"Well, how do we **get out** of here?" Rubix asked. "We're in the elfix stockroom. This is where we store the gifts before we deliver them on the **NIGHT OF THE DANCING STARS**. The bars are *narrow*, the walls are **solid**, and the ceiling is **HIGH**. It will be very **difficult** to get out of here without the key!"

Rubix was right! How were we going to escape?

"One of my many **inventions** would be helpful now, but they're all on the spaceship," Professor Greenfur said with a sigh.

"Wait a minute," Thea said suddenly, **pricking up** her ears. "I just heard something!"

"Huh?" I replied. "I didn't hear anything."

Ba-bump . . . Ba-bump . . . Ba-bump . . .

Holey craters! It sounded like pawsteps, and they were coming closer! **Who** could it be? Negativix? A guard?

"Is someone there?" I asked, my voice **TREMBLING** with fear.

"**UNCLE G**, it's us!" a little voice replied. I would have **recognized** that squeak anywhere.

"Benjamin! Bugsy Wugsy!" I squeaked. "You're safe! How did you get away from the **nebulos**?"

"It wasn't hard at all," Bugsy Wugsy *explained*. "The nebulos never even **SAW** us! As soon as they captured you, we ran behind a small house. When they took you away, we **went back** to the space pod and hid in a **SECRET** compartment."

"Then the nebulos took control of the space pod," Benjamin continued. "They drove it to a gigantic garage and searched through it. But we were so well hidden they couldn't find us! We waited for them to go away. Then we got out and followed them **down here**, where we found you!"

"Now we'll break you out of there!"

Bugsy Wugsy cried confidently.

"But how?!" Trap asked, unconvinced.

I looked at Benjamin and realized he was holding a small bag. He opened it and took out the **Tail Twister 2000**!

"Professor Greenfur, did you bring the Tail Twister 2000 on the space pod?!" I asked, surprised.

"Of course!" he replied. "You never know when your tail might need a **NEW LOOK**! Plus, I figured it might come in handy."

Benjamin nodded in agreement.

"I thought I might be able to use the Tail Twister 2000 to cut, curl, shave, or twist these bars!"

Mousey meteorites, Benjamin was right! The Tail Twister 2000 was a powerful tool, and it just might work. In any case, it was worth a try!

The blades were very **sharp** — no wonder it had **hurt** my tail so much! In no time at all, the Tail Twister 2000 had cut through the **BARS** of the cell.

"Thank you, my friends!" Rubix shouted happily.

I **hugged** my nephew tightly.

"Excellent work, Benjamin!" I squeaked. "But our **adventure** isn't over yet: We still have to rescue the other elfix!"

"Well said, Captain," Thea agreed. "Spacemice to the rescue!"

WHERE DO YOU THINK YOU'RE GOING?

We hurried down the hallway as QUICKLY as we could. Then we came to a large **wooden** door that was shut tightly.

"Everyone line up behind me," I instructed my friends, trying to keep my whiskers from shaking with fear. Then I opened the door a crack, trying to be as quiet as a mouse.

Suddenly, Professor Greenfur sneezed loudly:

Achoooooooo!

"Shhh!" Thea whispered. "Professor Greenfur, please try to restrain yourself."

"I'm so sorry!" the professor squeaked. "I just caught such a bad COLD on the ride here."

Then he blew his nose loudly, making even more noise! Plutonian Parmesan! If he kept this up, the nebulos aliens would find us for sure! I opened the door wider and saw a long, dark hallway. We moved forward SLOWLY,

our tails against the wall.

Suddenly, a loud **THUD** made us all

JUMP.

Rubix stepped forward.

"I'll go first, Captain," he volunteered. "I know this place well. We're in the hallways that lead to the elfix **toy laboratory**. That's where the nebulos aliens are keeping my friends as prisoners!"

We followed **Rubix** through a maze of hallways. We had to hurry. The nebulos could arrive at any moment!

Rubix turned *right*, then **left**, then *right* one more time.

"Follow me, quickly!" he said.

"Doesn't this hallway ever **end**?" Trap complained, panting. "When are we going to get there?"

"SHHH!" I hissed at my cousin. "Lower your *squeak*! Do you want us to get caught?"

He sighed. "Come on, G, lighten up," Trap said. "Can't you see that this hallway is **DESERTED**?"

Trap began to **skip** down the hallway, far ahead of us.

"See?" he said. "There's no one else here! Wheeee!"

"Trap, what are you doing?" I squeaked. "**Be careful!**"

But he wasn't listening to me.

"Let's keep close to him," Thea said, worried. "I don't want him to get into **trouble**!"

I ran ahead to **catch up** with Trap. When I reached him, I turned around to reassure my friends that everything was

fine. But instead of **smiling** back at me, Thea, Professor Greenfur, Bugsy Wugsy, Benjamin, and Rubix looked like they had just seen a **pirate spacecat**!

What was the matter?

When I turned back around, I understood immediately: **TRAP** was facing an enormouse creature with dark gray paws, a

humongous head, and two small, dark, **ENRAGED** eyes.

It was Negativix, and his nebulos friends were right *behind* him!

"Where do you think you're going, spacemice?" he growled menacingly.

WE WERE iN tROUBLE . . . again!

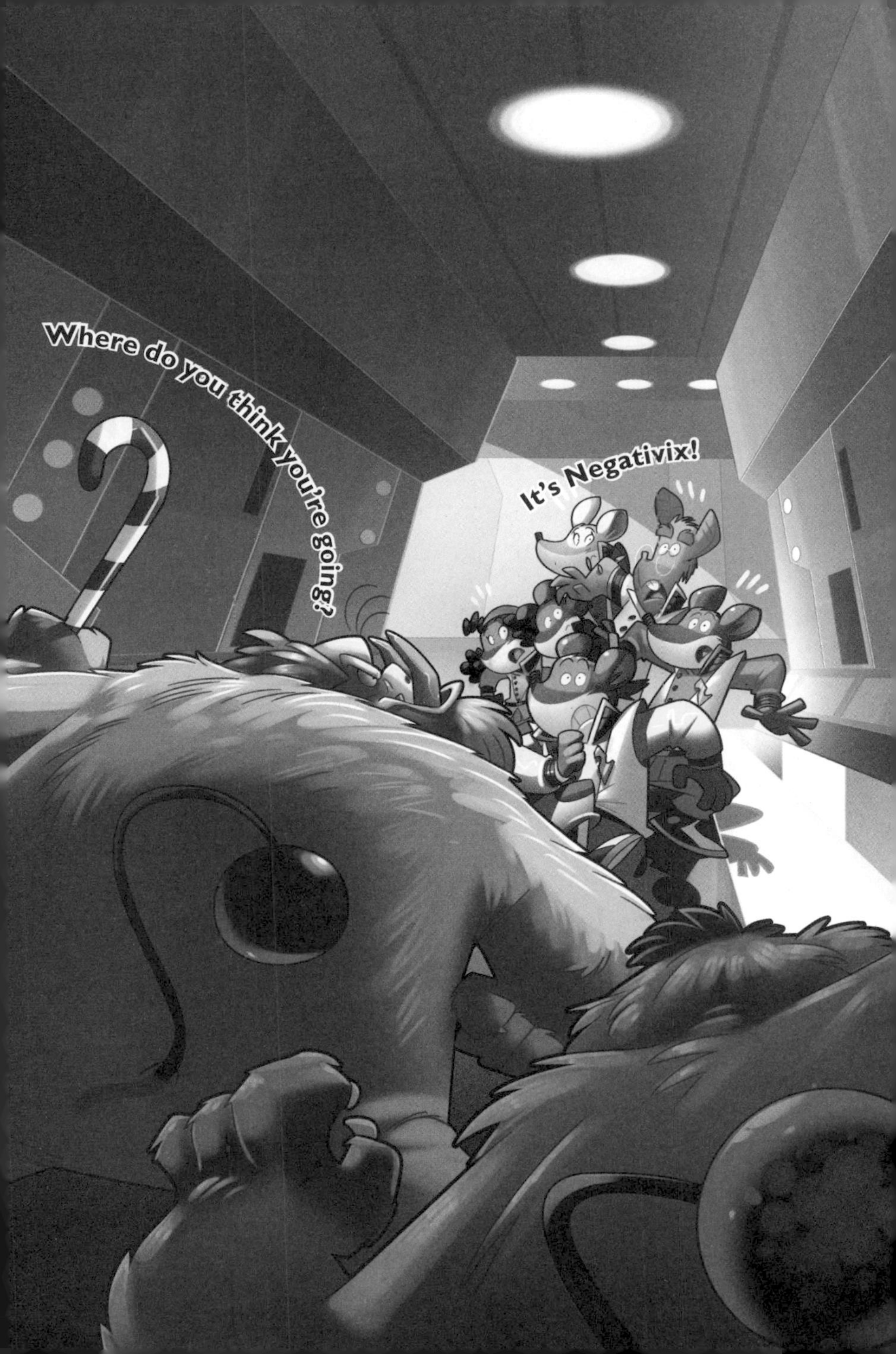
Where do you think you're going?
It's Negativix!

ALL YOU NEED IS A GOOD LAUGH . . .

Nebulos aliens began POPPing ouʈ from every doorway in the hallway.

"Catch them, guards!" Negativix ordered.

"Shake a tail, spacemice!" Thea shouted.

We all began to run in the opposite direction, sprinting through the MAZE of hallways. But the nebulos were right on our tails.

"**You'll never get away!**" Negativix shouted.

But we had almost **outrun** the nebulos when I suddenly slipped on a *toy* that had been lying on the floor. Here's what happened:

1. I tripped and *SLIPPED* . . .

2. I **bumped** into Trap and dragged him — and everyone else — down with me . . .

3. We all **HIT** the floor with a thud.

Professor Greenfur scrambled to get to his paws, rubbing his tail.

"Oh no!" he squeaked as he stood. "It's all over!"

The nebulos had just caught up with us. We were **G O N E R S** for sure!

But then something unexpected happened. The *expression* on Negativix's fangy face changed. Instead of looking angry, he looked amused! His mouth seemed to grow **larger** and **larger** and **larger** until he finally burst out laughing!

"HAHAHAHAHAHAHAHAHAHA!

How funny!" he exclaimed. "You bunch are really, really funny! Ha, ha, ha! Ho, ho, ho! Hee, hee, hee!"

Then something really weird happened: The small **dark** ball at the tip of his tail began to **glow**!

How strange! Once Negativix began to laugh, his tail glowed with a **GOLDEN** light and his fur became bright and **colorful** instead of dull and **gray**. Was it possible that the **dark** ball at the tip of each alien's tail was related to their **negative** thoughts?

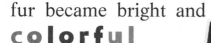

The other nebulos aliens stared at their leader, unsure of what to do. It seemed as if they had NEVER seen him laughing like that!

Negativix was completely doubled over. As he giggled, his fur kept changing — from gray to *BLUE* to **purple** to YELLOW to green!

His friends began to giggle, too. Suddenly, I knew *EXACTLY* what we needed to do: We had to make all the aliens LAUGH! So Thea and I started DANCING and jumping, and Trap began his favorite activity: telling jokes!

"*How do you know when the moon has had enough to eat?*" my cousin asked.

Negativix shook his head. "Um, I don't know!" he replied.

"**WHEN it's FULL!**" Trap cried.

The aliens all burst out laughing. "**HAHAHAHAHAAAAAAAAAA!**"

As they laughed, their tails began to glow, their fur changed **COLORS**, and their faces grew happier. It was clear the nebulos were changing: They weren't SCARY or **DANGEROUS** anymore!

HA! HA! HA! HA! HA! HA! HA! HA! HA! HA! HA! HA! HA! HA! HA! HA! HA! HA! HA! HA! HA! HA! HA! HA! HA! HA! HA! HA! HA! HA! HA! HA! HA! HA!

NEW FRIENDS

After a few minutes, the **nebulos** finally stopped laughing. Then a **blue**-and-**purple** Negativix gave me an enormouse hug.

"Thank you for saving us!" he said, tearing up as he spoke. "Before we met the spacemice, we were so **unhappy**."

"Oh, you're welcome," I replied,

Thank you!

turning as red as a cheese rind with **embarrassment**. "It was no big deal."

"That's not true!" Negativix said. "With your help, we nebulos realized that being **good** and GENEROUS is better than being **bad** and *envious*! Now we're all colorful, happy, and full of **JOY**! And we can't wait to apologize to the elfix."

Then he led us to the toy lab, where a festive crowd of happy elfix greeted us. While we spacemice had been busy making the nebulos laugh, Rubix had run ahead to **free** his friends!

"We are so sorry for taking you prisoner!" Negativix told the elfix. "We wanted your presents because no one had ever given us GiFTS before. But now we understand that the **best** presents are spontaneous, heartfelt, and given with joy! Please **FOR&iVE** us."

"We forgive you!" Rubix replied. "And we're sorry we never saw your planet. From now on we will bring many presents to **Nebula**. Your joy, happiness, and friendship will keep your planet **COLORFUL** and clearly visible to the rest of the universe!"

Aren't friendship and **FORGIVENESS** wonderful things? I was touched by the elfix's generosity and compassion. Suddenly, I had a **fabumouse** idea!

"Tomorrow is the **NIGHT OF THE DANCING STARS**," I announced. "We're planning a huge party on our spaceship, **MouseStar 1**. The **elfix** will be our guests, but we would like to invite the nebulos to come, too! Actually, you will be

Nebula the way it was before . . .

Nebula after its transformation!

the **guests of honor**!"

"Thank you!" Negativix replied with a big smile. "We would be **happy** to come to your party, friends! But first we want to help the elfix make their **presents**. We feel bad about the way we treated them, and we want to make it up to them!"

Holey space cheese! What a great idea!

The elfix accepted the offer, and the nebulos got right to work. Soon the toy laboratory was a **BUSY**, happy place again as the nebulos and the elfix worked together, **side by side**.

READY FOR THE PARTY?

We left the 𝕖𝕝𝕗𝕚𝕩 and the **NEBULOS** at work, and Rubix offered to escort us back to our space pod.

Look at the purple frillies!

What beautiful flowers!

When we stepped outside the laboratory, we were all **squeakless**: The fog had lifted, and Twinklix was colorful and shiny again! There were bright colors everywhere, and my eyes were drawn to a field of amazing **purple** flowers.

"They're called purple frillies," Rubix explained. Then he picked a large bunch.

"They are *special* flowers: As soon as you pick one, another one blooms in its place! And they bloom for a long time. If you receive one as a gift, it's a sign of long-lasting friendship and sincere affection. Here, take these! They're the **perfect** gift for a special someone."

"Thank you!" I said, smiling at my new friend. Maybe I had finally found a gift for Sally!

"Good-bye," Rubix said. "Have a good trip, my friends. And see you soon . . . The **NIGHT OF THE DANCING STARS** is almost here!"

We waved good-bye and boarded our ship,

eager to head home. As we flew, I glanced back at Twinklix. It was SHINING again, just as it should be.

When we arrived at the *MouseStar 1*, the other spacemice happily welcomed us back. Even Grandfather William seemed NICER than usual.

"**Well done, Grandson,**" he squeaked. "You behaved like a TRUE captain. Now, is everything ready for the party?"

Stellar Swiss! I had to run back to my cabin to finish writing my speech!

THE DANCING STARS

The next evening, it was finally the *NIGHT OF THE DANCING STARS*. The spaceship was decorated, the atmosphere was festive, and the **Space Yum Café** was full of delicious dishes and every kind of **dessert**.

I had finished writing my speech and was just going over it when I heard the **joyous screams** from the other spacemice announcing the arrival of the elfix's **star sled**.

Galactic Gorgonzola! I had to **hurry** to welcome our friends!

Rubix led his fellow elfix off their star sled together with the nebulos. They all ran toward us, smiling and laughing. The nebulos carried enormouse **golden**

bags full of gifts into the decorated hall of the Space Yum Café. They were the **BEST** kind of presents because they came from their hearts!

Before I knew it, it was time for my speech. I cleared my throat **nervously**. I may be the captain, but I still hate SQUEAKING in front of large groups!

Here are the presents!

Best wishes!

Hooray!

Hooray!

"Welcome, elfix and nebulos!" I began. "On this special night, I would like to thank you all from the bottom of my heart. THANK YOU, elfix, for the thoughtful and beautiful presents you bring every year. We would ESPECIALLY like to thank you for reminding us that **love** and **generosity** are the most important gifts. Thank you also, nebulos, for joining us tonight and for reminding us that joy comes from kindness and selflessness."

The nebulos beamed back at me. I concluded:

"Giving a gift is a way to tell someone you are thinking of him or her! It doesn't matter if the gift is precious or expensive — what matters is that it comes from the heart!"

A warm round of applause broke out. **SHOOTING STARS!** I was moved by the **LOVE** and SUPPORt of my friends.

Then it was time to open the gifts! The elfix had given me a new bookshelf for my many books. How thoughtful!

"Geronimo, WE have a gift for you, too!" Negativix said. "I made it myself!"

"Thank you," I squeaked, not sure what to say. I was moved by the gesture, but I had no idea what it was!

"It's a **nebulos** ornament!" Negativix explained.

I smiled warmly at my friend and then gave him a hug.

"Thank you so much!" I told him. "I really like it."

Then I heard a loud voice behind me.

"Grandson, I have a gift for you, too!" Grandfather William said, handing me an **elegant** bow tie printed with a pattern of small planets.

"Me too, G!" Thea said, giving me a space tennis racket and a membership to *MouseStar 1*'s TECHNOGYM. I'm really not a sportsmouse, but my sister is always trying to get me to improve my health!

MOUSEY METEORITES! I had received so many thoughtful presents from my friends and family. I felt like the LUCKIEST mouse in the universe!

On that note, I presented Sally with a bunch of sweet-smelling purple frillies. "Thanks, Captain!" she said, smiling **brightly** at me.

I wanted to tell her how I felt about her, but at that moment, the stars began dancing **joyfully** in the clear night sky. Everyone rushed to the spaceship windows to watch.

What a fabumouse show!

Holey craters, I was so happy! Even though I hadn't told Sally about my feelings, my friends and family were all around me on the most **beautiful** night in the galaxy. And this, my dear readers, is the best gift of all: sharing special moments with the ones you **love**!

Don't miss any adventures of the Spacemice!

#1 Alien Escape

#2 You're Mine, Captain!

#3 Ice Planet Adventure

#4 The Galactic Goal

#5 Rescue Rebellion

#6 The Underwater Planet

#7 Beware! Space Junk!

#8 Away in a Star Sled

Up Next!

#9 Slurp Monster Showdown

Be sure to read all my fabumouse adventures!

#1 Lost Treasure of the Emerald Eye

#2 The Curse of the Cheese Pyramid

#3 Cat and Mouse in a Haunted House

#4 I'm Too Fond of My Fur!

#5 Four Mice Deep in the Jungle

#6 Paws Off, Cheddarface!

#7 Red Pizzas for a Blue Count

#8 Attack of the Bandit Cats

#9 A Fabumouse Vacation for Geronimo

#10 All Because of a Cup of Coffee

#11 It's Halloween, You 'Fraidy Mouse!

#12 Merry Christmas, Geronimo!

#13 The Phantom of the Subway

#14 The Temple of the Ruby of Fire

#15 The Mona Mousa Code

#16 A Cheese-Colored Camper

#17 Watch Your Whiskers, Stilton!

#18 Shipwreck on the Pirate Islands

#19 My Name Is Stilton, Geronimo Stilton

#20 Surf's Up, Geronimo!

#21 The Wild, Wild West

#22 The Secret of Cacklefur Castle

A Christmas Tale

#23 Valentine's Day Disaster

#24 Field Trip to Niagara Falls

#25 The Search for Sunken Treasure

#26 The Mummy with No Name

#27 The Christmas Toy Factory

#28 Wedding Crasher

#29 Down and Out Down Under

#30 The Mouse Island Marathon

#31 The Mysterious Cheese Thief

Christmas Catastrophe

#32 Valley of the Giant Skeletons

#33 Geronimo and the Gold Medal Mystery

#34 Geronimo Stilton, Secret Agent

#35 A Very Merry Christmas

#36 Geronimo's Valentine

#37 The Race Across America

#38 A Fabumouse School Adventure

#39 Singing Sensation

#40 The Karate Mouse

#41 Mighty Mount Kilimanjaro

#42 The Peculiar Pumpkin Thief

#43 I'm Not a Supermouse!

#44 The Giant Diamond Robbery

#45 Save the White Whale!

#46 The Haunted Castle

#47 Run for the Hills, Geronimo!

#48 The Mystery in Venice

#49 The Way of the Samurai

#50 This Hotel Is Haunted!

#51 The Enormouse Pearl Heist

#52 Mouse in Space!

#53 Rumble in the Jungle

#54 Get into Gear, Stilton!

#55 The Golden Statue Plot

#56 Flight of the Red Bandit

Special Edition!

The Hunt for the Golden Book

#57 The Stinky Cheese Vacation

#58 The Super Chef Contest

#59 Welcome to Moldy Manor

Special Edition!

The Hunt for the Curious Cheese

#60 The Treasure of Easter Island

#61 Mouse House Hunter

#62 Mouse Overboard!

Special Edition!

The Hunt for the Secret Papyrus

#63 The Cheese Experiment

#64 Magical Mission

#65 Bollywood Burglary

MEET
Geronimo Stiltonord

He is a mouseking — the Geronimo Stilton of the ancient far north! He lives with his brawny and brave clan in the village of Mouseborg. From sailing frozen waters to facing fiery dragons, every day is an adventure for the micekings!

#1 Attack of the Dragons

#2 The Famouse Fjord Race

#3 Pull the Dragon's Tooth!

Don't miss any of these exciting Thea Sisters adventures!

Thea Stilton and the Dragon's Code

Thea Stilton and the Mountain of Fire

Thea Stilton and the Ghost of the Shipwreck

Thea Stilton and the Secret City

Thea Stilton and the Mystery in Paris

Thea Stilton and the Cherry Blossom Adventure

Thea Stilton and the Star Castaways

Thea Stilton: Big Trouble in the Big Apple

Thea Stilton and the Ice Treasure

Thea Stilton and the Secret of the Old Castle

Thea Stilton and the Blue Scarab Hunt

Thea Stilton and the Prince's Emerald

Thea Stilton and the Mystery on the Orient Express

Thea Stilton and the Dancing Shadows

Thea Stilton and the Legend of the Fire Flowers

Thea Stilton and the Spanish Dance Mission

Thea Stilton and the Journey to the Lion's Den

Thea Stilton and the Great Tulip Heist

Thea Stilton and the Chocolate Sabotage

Thea Stilton and the Missing Myth

Thea Stilton and the Lost Letters

Thea Stilton and the Tropical Treasure

Thea Stilton and the Hollywood Hoax

Thea Stilton and the Madagascar Madness

Meet
GERONIMO STILTONOOT

He is a cavemouse — Geronimo Stilton's ancient ancestor! He runs the stone newspaper in the prehistoric village of Old Mouse City. From dealing with dinosaurs to dodging meteorites, his life in the Stone Age is full of adventure!

#1 The Stone of Fire

#2 Watch Your Tail!

#3 Help, I'm in Hot Lava!

#4 The Fast and the Frozen

#5 The Great Mouse Race

#6 Don't Wake the Dinosaur!

#7 I'm a Scaredy-Mouse!

#8 Surfing for Secrets

#9 Get the Scoop, Geronimo!

#10 My Autosaurus Will Win!

#11 Sea Monster Surprise

#12 Paws Off the Pearl!

#13 The Smelly Search

Don't miss any of my adventures in the Kingdom of Fantasy!

THE KINGDOM OF FANTASY

THE QUEST FOR PARADISE:
THE RETURN TO THE KINGDOM OF FANTASY

THE AMAZING VOYAGE:
THE THIRD ADVENTURE IN THE KINGDOM OF FANTASY

THE DRAGON PROPHECY:
THE FOURTH ADVENTURE IN THE KINGDOM OF FANTASY

THE VOLCANO OF FIRE:
THE FIFTH ADVENTURE IN THE KINGDOM OF FANTASY

THE SEARCH FOR TREASURE:
THE SIXTH ADVENTURE IN THE KINGDOM OF FANTASY

THE ENCHANTED CHARMS:
THE SEVENTH ADVENTURE IN THE KINGDOM OF FANTASY

THE PHOENIX OF DESTINY:
AN EPIC KINGDOM OF FANTASY ADVENTURE

THE HOUR OF MAGIC:
THE EIGHTH ADVENTURE IN THE KINGDOM OF FANTASY

THE WIZARD'S WAND:
THE NINTH ADVENTURE IN THE KINGDOM OF FANTASY

MouseStar I

The spaceship, home, and refuge of the spacemice!

MouseStar I
(exterior view)

1. Control room
2. Gigantic telescope
3. Greenhouse to grow plants and flowers
4. Library and reading room
5. Astral Park, an amousement park
6. Space Yum Café
7. Kitchen
8. Liftrix, the special elevator that moves between all floors of the spaceship
9. Computer room
10. Crew cabins
11. Theater for space shows
12. Warp-speed engines
13. Tennis court and swimming pool
14. Multipurpose technogym
15. Space pods for exploration
16. Cargo hold for food supply
17. Natural biosphere

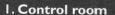

Dear mouse friends,
thanks for reading,
and good-bye until the next book.
See you in outer space!